the birth of a
humpback whale

the birth of a humpback whale

by robert matero

illustrated by
pamela johnson

atheneum books for young readers

Atheneum Books for Young Readers
An imprint of Simon & Schuster Children's Publishing Division
1230 Avenue of the Americas
New York, New York 10020

Book design by Angela Carlino
The text of this book is set in Goudy.
The illustrations are rendered in pencils.

Manufactured in the United States of America
First edition

10 9 8 7 6 5 4 3 2 1

Library of Congress Cataloging-in-Publication Data

Matero, Robert.
Birth of a humpback whale / by Robert Matero ; illustrated by Pamela Johnson.
p. cm.
Includes bibliographical references and index.
ISBN 0-689-31931-2
1. Humpback whale—Juvenile literature.
[1. Humpback whale. 2. Whales.] I. Johnson, Pamela, ill. II. Title.
QL737.C424M38   1995
599.5'1—dc20   94-10681

To Lydia and Nikaya, with all my love
—R. M.

To Anthony and Adriel, my beloved whale watching partners
—P. J.

Contents

the birth of a

humpback whale

Humpback Whales

Millions of years ago several groups of land-dwelling mammals, probably in search of food, and unlike any we would recognize today, waded into the shallow waters at the edge of the sea.

These first steps into water began the successful evolution of what was to become the whale from a land mammal to a marine mammal. It took sixty million years of gradual bodily changes, but today whales have so completely adapted to their watery world that they no longer resemble their four-legged ancestors that once roamed the earth.

Parts of the whale that were no longer useful to it eventually disappeared. Its nostrils moved back and up from the snout to the top of the head between the eyes, and turned into blowholes. These blowholes are connected directly to the whale's lungs, so that it can hunt and eat underwater. The whale developed a streamlined shape—perfect for life in the sea—insulated by a layer of blubber, or fat, instead of fur. Its hind legs disappeared, front legs developed into pectoral fins or flippers, and its tail evolved into a pair of gigantic

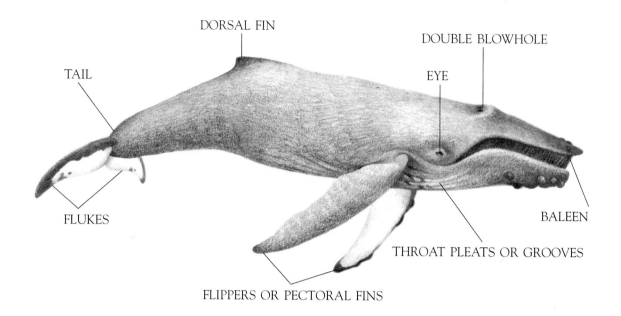

DORSAL FIN

DOUBLE BLOWHOLE

TAIL

EYE

FLUKES

BALEEN

THROAT PLEATS OR GROOVES

FLIPPERS OR PECTORAL FINS

flukes. Gradually, changes in each new generation produced a body more like that of a fish.

Most probably the whale's land-dwelling ancestors had teeth, which some species kept. In other species, called baleen whales, such as the humpback, the teeth were replaced by hundreds of plates of baleen.

Humpbacks belong to the whale family called rorquals or "pleated" whales. These "pleats" are actually deep grooves on the underside of the whale's body, which extend from the lower jaw to the belly.

Rorquals, like all baleen whales, have hundreds of flexible baleen plates, which grow downward from the whale's upper jaw. Baleen is made of keratin, the same material as our fingernails, and like fingernails keeps growing throughout the whale's life. These plates allow the humpback to feast on a tiny but abundant source of food—krill.

As a humpback feeds, its "pleated" throat expands like the folds of an accordion to form a large pouch, allowing it to gulp thousands of gallons of food and icy seawater in a single mouthful. Closing its mouth, the whale brings up its huge tongue (weighing close to two tons) and forces the water out between gray baleen plates. These plates act like a kind of strainer through which the seawater is filtered, trapping the krill on the fringed inner edges of the baleen—ready to be swallowed.

At times when food is less abundant, the whale's hunger takes it deep below the surface. Whales prepare for these sounding dives by taking a series of deep breaths, increasing the amount of oxygen taken into their lungs. The extra oxygen is stored in their blood and muscles. During these dives whales are able to slow down their heart-beats and limit the flow of blood to nonvital body parts. The whales' blood and muscle cells can then automatically release the stored oxygen to the vital areas of the brain and heart as needed, allowing them to remain underwater for long periods.

Although whales have a fishlike shape, they are not fish. Like dogs, horses, elephants, and humans, humpback whales are mammals: warm-blooded animals that breathe air through their lungs, give birth to live young, and nurse them with milk from the mother's body.

Whales are the largest animals the world has ever known; they are creatures of mystery—breathtaking, marvelous, and spectacular to behold—creatures whose existence makes our world a more exciting place.

To get to know these creatures, we have to go where few have gone before—to the undersea world of the humpback whale.

Humpbacks are born travelers. Their bony skeleton is light and spongy, making them nearly weightless in water. Their smooth, thin skin secretes an oily substance over their tapered bodies to reduce drag and their enormous bodies are able to slice through the oceans easily.

Humpbacks travel to the rich polar waters in the summer to feed and build up fat reserves. Newly pregnant females start to swim north to the polar feeding grounds first so that they are able to spend the longest amount of time there. Males and nonbreeding females follow. Though they travel in widely scattered small groups to reduce the risk of attack from sharks and killer whales (orcas), they are able to communicate with one another over miles of vast ocean with clicking sounds and whistles.

As winter approaches, hundreds of humpback whales and calves migrate from the frigid polar waters to share the warmer tropical seas near the equator. Since newborn whales lack the thick layer of blubber under their paper-thin skin to keep them warm, these mild, sheltered waters offer the perfect environment for the next generation of humpback babies to begin life.

Originally it was thought that humpbacks had fixed migration patterns, but new evidence suggests that some whales may travel widely over the ocean, eventually joining with one of the three distinct humpback whale populations: in the North Pacific, the North Atlantic, and those that swim in the waters of the southern hemisphere. A fourth population—those in the Arabian Sea—appear to remain there year-round.

In finding their way through all the world's oceans, the whales

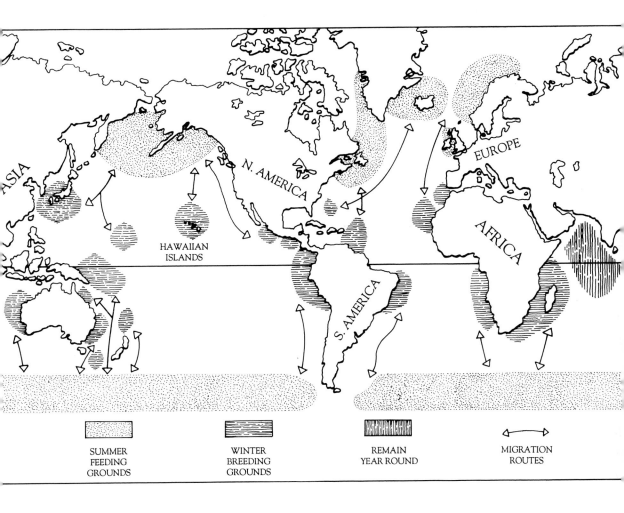

ASIA

N. AMERICA

EUROPE

AFRICA

S. AMERICA

HAWAIIAN
ISLANDS

SUMMER FEEDING GROUNDS	WINTER BREEDING GROUNDS	REMAIN YEAR ROUND	MIGRATION ROUTES

may be retracing the route passed on from one generation of humpbacks to another, following the underwater highways and currents.
Perhaps, as do other migrating animals, they use the sun, moon, and
stars as guides. Or does the information lie sleeping in their memory,
simply to be reawakened and used when needed? For now it remains
the humpbacks' secret.

2

A Baby Is Born

Close to the shore, in the early morning shadow of a steep cliff, a herd of humpbacks splashes and plays. Suddenly, forty tons of whale hurtles skyward twisting in midair, its long white flippers outstretched like the soaring wings of an eagle, before it falls back to the sea in an explosion of glittery spray.

Over and over the young male (bull) hurls himself acrobatically from the water inviting competition from other males and attracting the attention of interested females.

Other bulls take up his challenge—splashing, jumping, slamming the water with their huge tails.

After awhile the young bull takes off and joins a young female (cow). Humpback bulls must sometimes fight one another for the right to escort a female and, it is hoped, to mate with her. This time there is no rival's challenge and soon the pair begin to eagerly stroke each other with their huge flippers. Courtship among humpback whales is both playful and affectionate. Embracing, the pair rise—

belly to belly, heads high above the surface—their long, knobby flippers holding them upright as they mate.

Eleven months later the now-pregnant female returns to these same warm waters to become a mother for the first time. Oblivious to the boisterous courtship displays, she swims away from the herd to a small, protected lagoon off the western coast of the Hawaiian

island of Maui. The baby has been growing inside her—safe, floating, warm—and is now ready to come out to live on its own. The young female has begun labor; her uterus is contracting to push the baby out. A group of females, acting as midwives, swim close by to help if needed. It is a time of expectation—this mysterious moment of birth—an event as old as time, yet forever new. Before long, the baby's tail begins to emerge. Unlike the majority of land mammals, most whales are born tail first—an important advantage toward survival to a newborn suddenly emerging into an airless sea. Delivery is rapid. With the emergence of the calf's head the umbilical cord is pulled taut and separates. For the first few seconds the baby is helpless. Without air in her lungs the calf cannot breathe underwater. Her

mother quickly guides her to the surface for her first vital breath of air.

The newborn baby weighs over two tons and is fourteen feet long. Whales are able to deliver such large babies because their bodies are buoyed up by the salt water and by their thick layers of blubber.

The mother stays by her baby's side as she inhales her first breath of sea air. It is important for the newborn to develop the correct rhythm of breathing and blowing or else she could breathe in water, choke, and drown.

Through the warm turquoise water the newborn swims—awkwardly at first—at her mother's side. A smaller version of her mother, her rounded body is similar in both shape and color—dark gray on her upper body, while her throat, chest, and the undersides of her long flippers are white. The pepper-and-salt markings on the undersides of her tail flukes are as unique to her as fingerprints are to human beings.

The calf's arrival is an important event—a guarantee that the herd will continue.

The attendant midwives share in the joy of her first breath of life and accompany mother and child as they glide under a deep blue sky. All the adults share in the protection of their newest member and

position the baby between themselves and the nearby shore. This is done to shield her from the sharks and packs of killer whales that roam the seas preying upon the young and those that are very old, weak, or sick.

By swimming close to her mother, the baby learns how to breathe and swim on her own. She hovers just above her mother's back and steers herself by rotating her long flippers. Like a pair of synchronized swimmers, the movements of mother and child are perfectly coordinated.

After inhaling, the pair glide underwater, their double blowholes, or nostrils, closed tightly to form a watertight seal. With time, the baby will be able to inhale enough air at one breath to inflate over two hundred eleven-inch balloons. As the pair surface, the blowholes are exposed first. *Whoosh!* Powerful muscles raise their blowholes above the level of their heads, enabling them to exhale their hot breath into an eight- to twelve-foot-high geyserlike mist of spray shaped like a low, bushy tree.

This sudden explosion of air is mostly water vapor, but also includes some mucus and drops of oil. As it strikes the cooler outside air, it forms this visible plume, similar to when you "see your breath" on a cold day. Whalemen term this spouting or blowing.

All this work has made the baby hungry. Like all mammals, this young whale drinks her mother's milk. However, nursing underwater in the ocean is tricky. Instinctively, the baby approaches from the back, because her mother's nipples are enclosed in slits near her tail. As her mother rolls on her side to let her baby nurse, strong muscles push her nipples through these openings and she supports her infant with her long flippers. As the infant nuzzles up to the teat, her mother contracts the muscles surrounding the nipple and quickly

squirts a thick, satisfying stream of milk into her baby's mouth. Whale milk is said to taste both fishy and oily, but the newborn loves it! Swallowing, the baby returns to the surface for air. Since the new baby can't hold her breath for long, she feeds quickly and often—a few seconds at a time, about forty times a day!

The milk a whale baby receives from its mother is very rich in protein and minerals. Whale mothers convert part of their blubber into this nourishing milk for their infants. With an almost 50 percent fat content, it is more like heavy cream than the cow's milk we are used to drinking. The baby gulps the equivalent of 1,920 eight-ounce glasses a day of this rich, concentrated liquid, gaining over one hundred pounds per day (over four pounds an hour!). Such glut-

tony enables her to quickly acquire her own thick layer of blubber to insulate her and keep her warm in the cold waters ahead and to make her buoyant. Her mother, however, feeds very little during this time. Her blubber will sustain both her and her hungry baby until spring when they will migrate together to the polar waters for the first time to feed.

Nursing helps to form a close bond between mother and baby. Surfacing, they affectionately stroke each other with their huge flippers. Tired and content, they rest quietly at the surface, blending with the rhythm of the sea, its gentle rolling lulling them to sleep floating beneath a deep blue sky.

During the first few weeks the newborn calf requires constant attention. In the shallow water of the lagoon the baby never wanders far from her mother's watchful eyes, sometimes wriggling onto her broad back to rest as she lazes just beneath the surface of the water. The young calf loves to play and mother's tail makes the perfect slide. Repeatedly, she slips down her mother's wide, muscular flukes splashing joyfully in the gentle blue ripples. Occasionally, if she feels she's not getting enough attention, she covers her mother's blow-holes with her tail.

3

Growing and Learning

Sometimes the young mother leaps majestically from the water, cascading droplets that glitter in midair, and twists onto her back before smacking the surface with a thunderous boom, showering her baby in a glistening spray. Humpbacks are very playful and this activity, called breaching, seems contagious. Others in the nursery follow, exploding from the sea. All this is not lost on the young humpback, who quickly attempts to imitate the adults' behavior. Children learn through play and repetition and whale calves are no exception. Jumping with all her strength, the baby emerges halfway out of the water before landing on her throat, her small tail patting the surface softly.

With practice and added strength, the growing calf will soon master this valuable skill. For, in addition to being playful exercise, breaching may provide the whales a way to communicate their location to others in the pod or warn of danger; it may be used to show off strength to rivals, and as a means of removing itchy parasites, such as barnacles or whale lice, that attach themselves to their skin.

Gulls wheel through the air over ocean and beach, soaring

majestically, then dropping, riding the currents, seesawing in the light breeze as mother leads her daughter from the clear, shallow waters of the nursery and toward the mouth of the lagoon where the stronger currents flow. The pair stream back and forth through the currents, building their strength. The next few months will be extremely busy. Here under the watchful eyes of her mother the young calf will learn to use her body to convey messages and practice more of the important humpback whale skills that she will need for her long upcoming journey.

Pitching forward, her mother hangs head down in the water and

lashes her broad flukes from side to side, building momentum, and churning the water into white froth. With tremendous force she slaps her tail down against the foam to produce a thunderous crack that carries over a mile away. The young calf joins in.

Following their cue, nearby pod members soon fill the warm sea air with sharp, explosive claps. These lobtailing humpbacks may be sending messages to one another, venting their anger, or simply playing a game.

Like most young animals, the growing calf is extremely curious. Increasingly she leaves her mother for brief periods to explore the vast, watery world that is her home.

Her lengthening flippers send her gliding toward a group of other young humpbacks. A young male surges forward and rams her with his broad head—inviting her to play. Play is boisterous and high-spirited as the calves dive, twist, chase, and bump each other in their ocean playground. Touching is an important part of a whale's life and these young whales enjoy rubbing their new playmates with their flippers to become better acquainted.

Nearby, an older male whooshes noisily to the surface and looks around, motionless, his head and knobby chin shimmering under the brilliant midday sunshine. By hanging vertically in the water the humpback acts as a "lookout" for the other pod members. Quietly dipping below the surface, he rises again, eyeing his surroundings once more. This is known as spy-hopping.

The young whales follow suit, mimicking the adult. Suddenly the young calf realizes how hungry she is. Racing away, she rejoins her mother, rubbing against her large gray body, her familiar touch soothing and reassuring. Turning sleepily, the whale baby gulps the rich milk.

Content and tired, she dozes alongside her mother on gently rolling swells.

Mother and daughter awake refreshed. They glide in unison through the warm water. The currents carry to them an extraordinary series of long, slow sounds—a complex combination of whistles, groans, clicks, gurgles, and squeaks. The music is eerie and beautiful, and beckons them. Instinct and curiosity move them forward.

Nearly motionless below the surface, the soloist—his head lowered, flippers outstretched, large body angled downward—serenades the nearby females. The melodies are created by bursts of air coming from inside his head, throat, and lungs.

Each "song" lasts from seven to thirty minutes and is composed of from two to six themes, which always follow each other in the same sequence.

The young male rises, spouts, then descends slowly. The song begins again, following the same pattern.

Soon his voice is joined by other bulls all singing the same song, but each beginning and ending at a different time, filling the darkening waters with a chorus of voices interweaving their wonderful variety of sounds.

These haunting underwater songs are sung to attract cows or warn rivals to stay away.

Although all the male humpbacks in a mating area sing the same song at the same time, the song is constantly changing. The song that ends one mating season is memorized and carried over to begin the next. As the season progresses, the whales begin tinkering—adding new variations, eliminating others—always changing, yet each whale learns and memorizes the changes so that they are all singing the new melody at the same time.

Human beings and humpback whales are the only mammals who are able to compose their own music.

All through the night the humpbacks perform. Their oceanic concert hall echoes with their original and beautiful compositions. Gradually the singing fades, as one by one the males leave to pursue the females. All is quiet.

The bright golden rim of the sun peeks over the horizon. In the

distance two large males challenge each other in a breaching contest
—their thunderous landings rolling and echoing over the lagoon,
shattering the quiet of dawn.

A stiff breeze brushes the water, putting curls of white on the
surface. The whale child and her mother break the surface swimming
slowly, their immense bodies gradually cutting through the choppy
blue water. Pausing to rest, the calf slips beneath the surface and
emerges with a floating patch of kelp perched atop her head—a sun-
bonnet of soggy green. The two play together with the new toy—
pushing, patting, scooping the seaweed with their flippers and tails.

The growing calf still has much to learn and soon her mother
swims ahead, her child trailing in her wake. The rest of the morning
is spent practicing diving, breaching, and lobtailing.

Angled up, the mother humpback and her calf surface into a forward roll and blow puffs of frosty breath. Six or seven rapid breaths are inhaled through their double blowholes to restore needed oxygen to their blood and muscles. In one fluid and graceful motion the blowholes snap tightly shut, the heads turn down, and their bodies lift out of the water and arch into the characteristic rounded hump from which the humpback whale derives its name. By flipping their

enormous flukes straight into the air the whales seem to stand on their heads before disappearing.

A flick of their tails propels mother and daughter deep into their dark and shadowed world. Greasy tears bathe their eyes, preventing the salty water from stinging them during these deep, or sounding dives.

After fifteen minutes the pair resurface and blow, their stale breath creating a cloud of shimmering spray, which drifts and dissipates quickly in the strong breeze.

Swimming forward, the young humpback suddenly rolls onto her right side and lifts her glistening black-and-white flipper into the air, waving it playfully as if to welcome the seesawing gulls.

The spring sun continues visible and warm. The mother humpback swims restlessly. She is hungry. There is not enough food in these warm tropical waters to satisfy her huge appetite. Since arriving here at the beginning of winter she has been living off her blubber and nourishing her baby from it. During this time her calf has nearly doubled in length (to about twenty-five feet) and now weighs close to eighteen tons!

Each day the warm lagoon grows quieter. Most of the whales have already begun their long swim north. Mother and daughter are among the last of the pod to leave. They linger as long as possible, building up the calf's strength for the difficult three thousand-mile journey.

Finally, instinct and her hunger tell the mother it is time. An upward stroke of their powerful tails starts them northward—their wakes whitening and broadening under a brilliant orange sun.

4

Journey North

Mother's and daughter's powerful horizontal flukes push up and down against the darkening blue-green water. Dorsal fin and flippers provide balance and stability as they plow forward through the vast cornerless expanse of water.

Daylight turns to darkness and back to daylight again. Days form into weeks. For three weeks they swim—a solitary pair—rising regularly to fill their lungs with the salty sea air. Since the whales will drown if they go into a deep sleep, they instead catnap near the surface, day or night, whenever tired—sometimes continuing to swim as they sleep, their mighty tails powering them forward.

The young mother swims slowly so as not to lose her baby. With a series of clicks and whistles she signals the other members in her traveling pod to slow down or speed up to match their pace. Lacking her mother's great strength and stamina, the calf sometimes hitches a ride on the backwash created by her mother, which helps to pull her through the white-capped waves.

Three o'clock—thick black clouds loom in the west. Overhead the sky has turned a darker, more ominous shade of gray.

An angry wind chases choppy waves capped in white across their paths. The mother humpback inhales the sea air—damp and chilly, promising rain—scenting trouble.

A deep rumble of thunder announces the rain. Plip—plip—plop. First drops, large and heavy, fall gently on the ocean, dimpling its surface. Soon the rain is falling in heavy sheets. The sky crackles and vibrates. Flickering zigzags of lightning stab down from the blackening sky, frightening the surfacing baby whale, who fights forward through the surging sea. Giant waves hurl and batter one another. Sheets of rain assault them.

The calf follows her mother to the calmer waters below the surface. Fifty feet down the going is still slow. Mother and daughter strain against the current. Desperate for air the pair rise to the surface.

Huge, powerful waves explode over them, smashing and pounding their bodies, covering their blowholes before they can close them fully, causing them to inhale water. The older whale recovers first, but her baby panics, breathing in more deeply. Sputtering, choking, she is pulled and carried down by the strength of the current, separating her from her mother.

Quickly her mother dives into the watery darkness, twisting right, then left. There—to her left—she senses her distressed child.

She surges forward, straining, her overworked lungs screaming for air. They touch. She has her baby! Lunging upward, she pushes her baby up, breaking the stormy surface, spouting, gasping, breathing, diving back down until a rhythmic breathing pattern returns. The young whale is frightened but unharmed.

All through the night the rain pelts down. Flashes of lightning rip through the sky bathing the sea in an eerie glow. The wet wind shrieks and roars, raking the surface, creating huge swells that hammer and punish their bodies as they rise for air, further sapping their strength.

Toward dawn the black sky turns gray. Gradually the rain dissolves into a misty drizzle, the wind quiets, and the ocean reclaims its smooth roll. A last echo of thunder wafts across a charcoal sky. Early morning fog rolls in from the west enfolding them in its misty

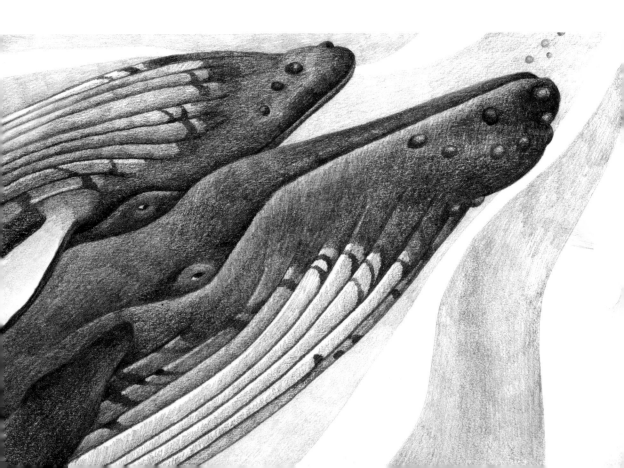

shroud. Exhausted, mother and calf sleep, side by side, reassured by each one's gentle touch. In sleep they instinctively rise to the surface to breathe without waking.

The lifting fog unveils a daylight raw, cold, blustery, with thick gray clouds hulking overhead.

Awake now, a powerful wave of their tails starts them northward again. As gusting winds from the north chill the spring morning, the dark clouds overhead drift apart uncovering a washed-out blue sky. The mother humpback senses their struggle has put them behind the

rest of their group and signals their location to them. Since sound travels at a rate of almost a mile per second underwater, her message is quickly carried to the other pod members.

Twenty-five miles away five great black-and-white bodies also hear her sounds, quickly veer, and spurt forward, cutting through the gray-green ocean, driven by their powerful hunger. These orcas, or killer whales, now send out high-pitched sound waves that bounce off the humpback pair and return like an echo, helping them identify and pinpoint their targets. This ability of toothed whales is called echolocation. Humpbacks, and other baleen whales, must rely on sight and sound to find food.

The strong currents carry the orcas' menacing clicks. Sensing their peril, the humpback mother smacks her flippers and flukes against the surface sending out a distress call. Five shadowy killers suddenly appear on her left.

Killer whales are fearless, and when food is scarce they will attack and kill whales many times their size.

Like wolves, killer whales hunt in packs, the members working together as a team. Combining the strength of many orcas enables them to attack and kill whales that would be too large for one alone.

The killers swim forward—cautiously—circling their prey, darting in and out, looking for a weakness, trying to isolate the young whale. The calf cowers closer for protection. Terrified, her mother rises up. Lashing out with her powerful tail, she smashes and stuns one of their hunters. Flashing razor-sharp teeth, a bold pair of orcas attack the flukes of the mother. Another tries to pry open the mother's mouth with its powerful jaws to tear out her tongue, knowing death will result. Knifing forward, one of the attackers rakes the mother's tail. Blood spurts—turning the water crimson. Ignoring her pain, she lashes out violently, beating the killers away with blows from her mighty tail, churning the sea into a red froth.

Fierce, aggressive, intelligent predators, the orcas quickly double back, separate, and move in, stalking the pair from many directions. One killer swims on either side to prevent escape, one swims beneath to block mother and daughter from diving to get away, and two killers swim above to keep the frightened humpbacks underwater, unable to surface, so they will drown.

Suddenly, the orcas attack, tearing at the mother's tail fin. She slashes out with her flukes slamming one killer back. The humpbacks dive to evade their attackers—tilting to the right, then the left, veering, thrashing their flukes, twisting, lunging, swirling—their agility and grace belying their great bulk.

Surging upward, mother and daughter charge toward light, air, life—breaking free—driving a killer whale from their path!

Other humpbacks now thunder toward the pair in response to their troubled call for help. The killers hesitate, then withdraw.

Mother and daughter rub against each other—thankful to have escaped their assailants. Inhaling the sea air, faintly salty, fresh, and cool, the humpbacks resume their polar migration. In time the mother's tail will heal, but she will carry her scars forever.

5

Arctic Summer

It is late spring. The traveling humpbacks rise regularly to refill their lungs with salt air. The small pod moves past large floes of sea ice that shimmer diamondlike under the slanted pink beams of the rising sun. The water is becoming increasingly cold and the young mother senses they are nearing the completion of their nearly two-month-long journey.

Suddenly, the older whales spurt ahead. They have spotted a reddening of the water that signals a surfacing school of krill, tiny shrimplike crustaceans, their favorite meal! The krill have come up to feed on the vast floating forests of kelp. This giant seaweed makes its food from sunlight and the nutrients in the ocean water.

The young calf watches her mother lunge forward, mouth open. After their long journey her mother and the other adult humpbacks are ravenous. With quick, shallow dives the whales stream back and forth through an enormous school of krill devouring millions of these protein-rich, finger-length crustaceans that abound in the cold polar waters. In addition to krill, small fish such as capelin, cod, her-

ring, and sand lance flourish, turning the ocean into a rich seafood chowder. The mother gulps over two tons of seafood per day, enough to feed a family of four human beings for a year. Much of this is converted to fat and stored. This enables her to quickly replenish her layer of blubber.

The krill try to escape being eaten by slipping under the surface to vanish into the black waters below. Flukes thrust high into the crisp air, the mother quickly follows.

A school of herring—silvery, shimmering, handsome—suddenly scatters from her path. The rounded head of an octopus scoots in front of her face. She pulls herself deeper with strong, sweeping strokes, past tall peaks of undersea mountains.

Here, in the icy blackness almost six hundred feet from the surface, vision is limited. But the whale's acute hearing enables her to detect the crackling sound of krill and target her prey. She zeros in, open-mouthed.

Surfacing with a loud whoosh, the mother spouts, then inhales deeply, her breath rushing into and refilling her lungs with a shrill whine, and swims alongside her baby—satisfied.

Feeling hungry, the young calf nudges her mother. For now, she is content to nurse, but as the summer advances, mother's milk will become saltier, losing its familiar pleasant taste, and the calf will begin to eat more and more of the nourishing krill. By the time the humpbacks begin their breeding migration to the tropics, she will probably be weaned.

The day is mild. A light summer breeze sweeps across the sea seasoning the air with a salty aroma. The young calf lolls peacefully, the warm sun on her back. With a thunderous splash her mother bursts through a rising "cloud" of bubbles forty feet away, her huge mouth overflowing with krill and fish.

Minutes later the mother plunges back down into the blue-green ocean releasing another cloud of tiny bubbles. This bubble cloud expands as it rises, camouflaging her as she pursues the thousands of krill and small fish being herded to the surface to be devoured. The young calf watches, another lesson in her continuing education.

Her mother dives again, deeper this time. Below the scattering school she swims upward in a slow spiral, exhaling from her blow-holes to form the bubbles. These rising columns of air bubbles form a circle or "net" that surrounds and traps her prey. The bubbles frighten the krill, which flee toward the center of the net and the security of the group. The whale lunges upward through the middle of the bubble-net, her huge mouth wide open, filtering thousands of tiny krill and fish from the icy seawater.

Two nearby humpbacks join her. Thrashing, turning, diving, spouting, they gorge themselves, quickly churning the watery circle to white froth.

The growing calf joins the adults, devouring hundreds of pounds of the surfacing food.

Above, a flock of opportunistic gulls hovers, watchful, waiting to snatch food from the whales' bubble-net as it surfaces.

This method of bubble feeding is unique to the humpback, and the young calf must learn and practice it in order to survive.

Here, in the cold-water feeding grounds, a large part of the humpbacks' day is spent eating, building up their strength and reserves of blubber. However, the young calves, as do all young animals everywhere, still find time to play—splashing, breaching, lobtailing—having great fun with one another in the endless daylight of the arctic summer.

Then one day a brisk late afternoon breeze blows up from the west pushing a gray cloud in front of the sun, which darkens the sky and chills the air. In the waning days of summer the humpbacks sense the ocean's changes—the water is colder, the food less plentiful.

Scarred flukes thrust high, the young mother plunges ninety feet, her large tail fin fanning up and down, and releases a steady stream of large bubbles. Delighted, her frisky calf splashes in them as they flow to the surface.

Dusk deepens, changing to dark. The late autumn breeze rakes the sea, and rising waves crest and hiss as they break, foaming white. The humpbacks swim restlessly back and forth amid the roiling breakers.

During the summer feeding months, the humpbacks had stopped "singing." Now some of the young bulls, anxious to mate, begin to sing again. Their song is the same as at the end of last year's breeding season, but their constant tinkering will revise it completely within a few years. These songs will continue until next spring's return to the feeding grounds.

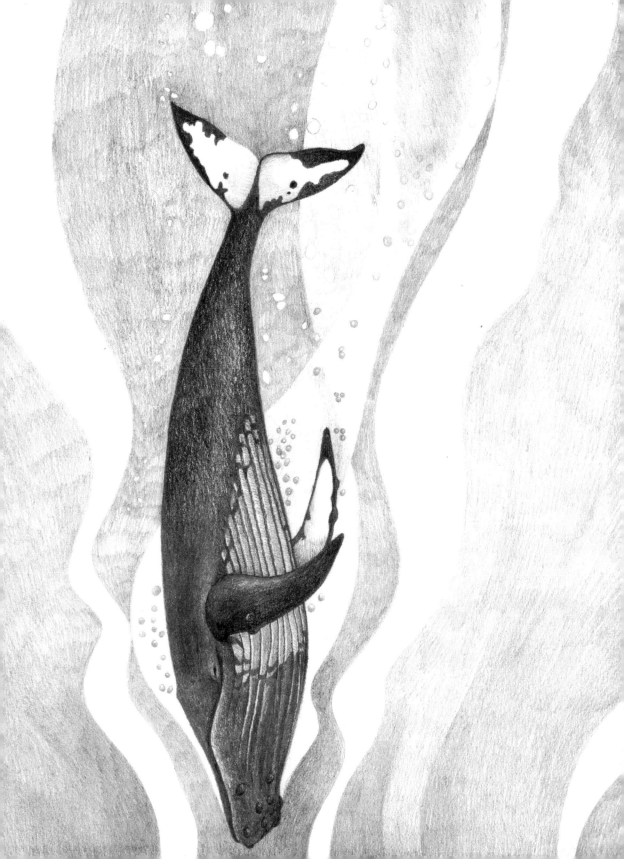

Tomorrow the young calf and her mother will begin the long retreat to the warmer equatorial waters. For the calf it will be the first of forty or more annual migrations to her mating and calving grounds.

In seven years she will be ready to mate and give birth to a baby of her own, thus ensuring new generations of these remarkable and magnificent creatures.

Afterword

Humpback whales have the power to excite the mind and stir the imagination. Nevertheless, each year a large number of humpbacks are hunted down and slaughtered because there is money to make by doing it. Their huge size makes them appear invincible, but unfortunately, that is not the case. In truth, their size works against them. Slow-moving with thick layers of oil-producing blubber, they make ideal targets for today's sophisticated and deadly whale-hunting techniques. Whale oil is used in making a wide variety of products from cosmetics to transmission oil for our cars. Today, however, these products can be made better and more efficiently using substitutions for whale oil, so that the mass destruction of these peaceful, intelligent mammals is completely unnecessary.

In addition, our coastal waters have become a dumping ground for toxic chemicals and garbage, which poison our oceans and further deplete the humpback population. Krill, the humpbacks' main source of protein, is now being harvested by many nations to feed those countries' expanding human and animal populations. This competition for food could eventually result in serious food shortages for the humpback, and its possible starvation.

The future of the humpback and of all the great whales depends on what we do. To ensure that the baby humpback and her children and grandchildren survive and are able to swim and play and feed the

way they were meant to, we must protect their world. People who care are working together to help save the whales. Following is a list of groups to write to, to find out what you can do. Please help. The whales are waiting—they cannot wait forever!

For More Information

Become a friend of the humpback and of all the great whales. For more information, please contact:

American Cetacean Society
P.O. Box 2639
San Pedro, CA 90731

Defenders of Wildlife
1244 Nineteenth Street, N.W.
Washington, DC 20036

Hubbs Sea World Research Institute
1700 South Shores Road
San Diego, CA 92109

International Whaling Commission
The Red House
Station Road
Histon
Cambridge CB4 4NP
England

Marine Mammal Commission
1625 Eye Street, N.W.
Washington, DC 20006

National Wildlife Federation
1400 Sixteenth Street, N.W.
Washington, DC 20036-2266

New York Aquarium
Osborn Laboratories of Marine Sciences
New York Zoological Society
Surf Avenue at West Eighth Street
Brooklyn, NY 11224

Rare Animal Relief Effort, Inc.
National Audubon Society
950 Third Avenue
New York, NY 10022

United States Department of Commerce
National Marine Fisheries Service
National Oceanic and Atmospheric
Administration
Washington, DC 20235

United States Department of the Interior
Fish and Wildlife Service
Washington, DC 20240

U.S. Navy's Marine Mammal Program
Naval Ocean Systems Center
San Diego, CA 92152

The Whale Center
3929 Piedmont Avenue
Oakland, CA 94611

The Whale Protection Fund
624 Ninth Street
Washington, DC 20001

World Wildlife Fund
1250 Twenty-fourth Street, N.W.
Washington, DC 20037

Places to Visit

American Museum of Natural History, New York, New York

Gray Whale Natural Park, Guerrero Negro, Mexico

Joseph M. Long Marine Laboratory, Santa Cruz, California

Kendall Whaling Museum, Sharon, Massachusetts

Mystic Marinelife Aquarium, Mystic, Connecticut

Nantucket Whaling Museum, Nantucket Island, Massachusetts

National Museum of Natural History, Washington, D.C.

Sag Harbor Whaling Museum, Sag Harbor, New York

Santa Barbara Museum of Natural History-Sea Center,
    Santa Barbara, California

Science Museum of Connecticut, West Hartford, Connecticut

Tale of the Whale Museum, New London, Connecticut

Whaling Museum, New Bedford, Massachusetts

Glossary

ancestor: an early type of animal from which later kinds have evolved.

baleen: a row of flexible plates or strips that hangs down from the whale's upper jaw and acts as a sieve, allowing water to filter out while trapping krill and small schooling fish.

barnacles: saltwater shellfish that attach themselves to ship bottoms, rocks, piers, and whales.

blow: when whales spout water, air, oil droplets, and mucus from the lungs into the air.

blowhole: the nostril of a whale. Humpbacks and other baleen whales have a double blowhole on the top of their heads; toothed whales have a single blowhole.

blubber: the thick layer of fat beneath the whale's skin.

breach: a whale's leap from the water and its landing.

bull: a male whale.

buoyant: being able to float.

calf: a young whale.

cow: a female whale.

crustaceans: any of a group of animals that live primarily in water, including shrimps, crabs, krill, and lobsters, with jointed legs and a segmented hard-shell body.

echolocation: a system of navigation based on sound. Toothed whales emit a series of sounds that strike an object and bounce back as echoes that are quickly analyzed, to provide information about the location, distance, and size of the objects in the whales' environment. Whales use echolocation to detect prey, navigate, and avoid obstacles.

escort: an adult bull that accompanies a cow in the warm-water breeding grounds.

evolution: the development of a species, organism, or organ from its original or primitive state to its present or specialized state.

flippers: broad, flat forelimbs of marine mammals used for steering and balancing their bodies as they swim.

flukes: a whale's horizontal tail is divided by a distinctive center notch into two halves called flukes, which are serrated and pointed at the tips.

herd: a group of wild or domestic animals that feed and travel together.

ice floe: a flat, free mass of floating sea ice.

instinct: an inborn tendency to behave in a way characteristic of a species.

krill: tiny shrimplike crustaceans.

mammals: any of a class of higher warm-blooded vertebrates that usually give birth to live young, nourish their young with milk from special glands in the mother's body, have some hair on their bodies, and have a four-chambered heart. Whales have only a few facial hairs.

migration: the seasonal movement of animals from one region to another and back again.

nurse: to feed young with milk secreted from the mammary glands in the mother's body.

nurseries: a place where young animals grow or are cared for.

parasites: small animals that live on or in another animal, such as a whale, which can be harmful.

pod: a group of from three to fifteen whales.

predator: an animal that hunts other animals for food.

prey: an animal being hunted for food.

rorquals: a species of baleen whales that have throat grooves or ridges which extend from its lower jaw to its belly.

teats: nipples through which milk passes in nursing the young.

toxic chemicals: poisonous chemicals that in large amounts can damage or destroy plant and animal life.

umbilical cord: a fibrous cord extending from the mother's uterus to the unborn baby. It contains blood vessels through which food and oxygen flow to the baby.

uterus: a hollow organ in most female mammals that protects and nourishes the developing baby until birth.

whale lice: small aquatic crustaceans that infest and live off certain species of whales.

For Further Reading and Listening

Bright, Michael. *Humpback Whales*. New York: Gloucester Press, 1990.

Bunting, Eve. *The Sea World Book of Whales*. San Diego: Harcourt, Brace, Jovanovich, 1980.

Cousteau, Jacques–Yves, and Yves Paccalet. *Whales*. New York: Harry N. Abrams, 1988.

Ellis, Richard. *The Book of Whales*. New York: Alfred A. Knopf, 1980.

Goldner, Kathryn Allen, and Carole Garbuny Vogel. *Humphrey the Wrong Way Whale*. Minneapolis: Dillon Press, 1987.

Green, Carl R., and William R. Sanford. *The Humpback Whale*. New York: Crestwood House, 1985.

McGovern, Ann. *Little Whale*. New York: Four Winds Press, 1979.

Nicklin, Flip, and Roger Payne. "New Light on Singing Whales." *National Geographic*, April 1982, pp. 463–477.

Payne, Roger S. "Humpbacks: Their Mysterious Songs." *National Geographic*, January 1979, pp. 18–25.

———. *Songs of the Humpback Whale*. Capitol Records, 1970.

Simon, Seymour. *Whales*. New York: Thomas Y. Crowell, 1989.

Slijper, Everhard J. *Whales*. Ithaca, N.Y.: Cornell University Press, 1979.

Time-Life Books, Editors of. *Whales and Other Sea Mammals*. New York: Time-Life Films, 1977.

Watson, Lyall. *Sea Guide to Whales of the World*. New York: E. P. Dutton, 1981.

Winn, Lois King, and Howard E. Winn. *Wings in the Sea: The Humpback Whale*. Hanover, N.H.: University Press of New England, 1985.

Index

D

Defenders of Wildlife, 42
Department of the Interior, U.S., 42
Dives, sounding, 3
Dorsal fin, 2, 24

E

Eating habits, 32–36
Echolocation, 29, 45
Educational places to visit, 43
Environmental organizations, 42
Equatorial migration, 4, 39
Escort, 45
Evolution, 1–2, 45

F

Fat. *See* Blubber
Feeding habits, 32–36
Female whales. See Cows
Flippers, 1, 2, 23, 24, 30, 45
Flukes, 2, 23, 24, 30, 45
Food shortages, 40

G

Gray Whale National Park, 43
Groups, environmental, 42
Gulls, 15–16, 23, 36

H

Hawaii, 7
Hearing ability, 34
Herd, 46
Herring, 32–33
Hubbs Sea World Research Institute, 42

Humpback whales
    anatomy of, 2–4
    birth of, 7–8
    evolution of, 1–2
    feeding by, 32–36
    human threats to, 40–41
    migration of, 4–5, 24–31, 39
    nursing of, 11–13, 35, 46
    origin of name for, 22
Hunting of whales, 40

I

Ice floes, 32, 46
Instinct, 46
International Whaling Commission, 42

J

Joseph M. Long Marine Laboratory, 43
Jumping, 15

K

Kelp, 21, 32
Kendall Whaling Museum, 43
Keratin, 2
Killer whales (orcas), 4, 11, 29–31
Krill, 3, 32–35, 40, 46

L

Learning process, 15–16, 18
Lice, whale, 15, 47
Lightning, 25, 27
Lobtailing, 18, 21, 36
"Lookout" function, 18

M

Male whales. *See* Bulls

Mammals, 1, 3, 46

Marine Mammal Commission, 42

Marine mammals, evolution of, 1-2

Mating songs, 20, 36

Maui, Hawaii, 7

Midwives, 8, 10

Migration, 4–5, 46

    arctic, 24–31

    equatorial, 4, 39

Milk, 11–12, 35

Museums, 43

Music, 19–20

Mystic Marinelife Aquarium, 43

N

Nantucket Whaling Museum, 43

National Audubon Society, 42

National Marine Fisheries Service, 42

National Museum of Natural History, 43

National Oceanic and Atmospheric Administration, 42

National Wildlife Federation, 42

Navy, U.S., Marine Mammal Program, 42

Newborn whales, 9–10

New York Aquarium, 42

Nipples, 11, 47

Nurseries, 46

Nursing, 11–13, 35, 46

O

Octopus, 33

Oil, whale, 40

Orcas. *See* Killer whales

P

Parasites, 15, 46

Pectoral fins, 1, 2

Playfulness, 14, 15, 18, 36

Pleated whales, 2

Pleats, 2, 3

Pod, 46

Polar migration, 24–31

Predators, 30, 47

Pregnancy, 7–8

Prey, 30, 47

R

Rare Animal Relief Effort, Inc., 42

Rorquals, 2, 47

S

Sag Harbor Whaling Museum, 43

Sand lance, 33

Santa Barbara Museum of National History-Sea Center, 43

Science Museum of Connecticut, 43

Seagulls, 15–16, 23, 36

Seaweed, 21, 32

Signaling, 24, 28–29

Singing, 20, 37

Skeleton, 4

Skin, 4

Slaughter of whales, 40

Sleeping habits, 24, 27

Songs, 20, 37

Sounding dives, 3

Organizations, environmental, 42

Osborn Laboratories of Marine Sciences, 42

Sounds, underwater, 28–29

Sound waves, 29

Speech. *See* Communications

Spouting. *See* Blowing

Spy-hopping, 18

Swimming, 11

T

Tail, 2, 30, 31

Tale of the Whale Museum, 43

Tears, 23

Teats, 11, 47

Throat pleats, 2, 3

Thunderstorm, 25–27

Tongue, 3, 30

Touching, 18

Toxic chemicals, 40, 47

U

Umbilical cord, 8, 47

Undersea mountains, 33

Underwater sounds, 20, 28–29

U.S. Department of Commerce, 42

U.S. Department of the Interior, 42

U.S. Navy's Marine Mammal Program, 42

Uterus, 8, 47

W

Weaning, 35

Weight gain, 12, 23

Whale Center, The, 42

Whale-hunting, 40

Whale lice, 15, 47

Whale oil, 40

Whale Protection Fund, The, 42

Whales

    evolution of, 1–2

    groups for protecting, 42

    human threats to, 40–41

    See also Humpback whales

Whaling Museum, 43

Whistles, 4, 24

World Wildlife Fund, 42